TO MY DOG FLOC,

my family, my friends, and all
the amazing people that I have
come to know this year.

First published in 2011 by Child's Play (International) Ltd
Ashworth Road, Bridgemead, Swindon SN5 7YD, UK

Distributed in USA by Child's Play Inc
250 Minot Avenue, Auburn, Maine 04210

Distributed in Australia by Child's Play Australia Pty Ltd
Unit 10/20 Narabang Way, Belrose, Sydney, NSW 2085

ISBN 978-1-84643-908-7
SJ210422CPL06229087

Printed and bound in Shenzhen, China

9 10 8

A catalogue record of this book is available from the British Library

www.childs-play.com

Marta Altés

Hi! MY NAME
IS <u>NO</u>.

I'm a ~~good~~ (very) good boy.
I AM SO GOOD THAT
MY FAMILY IS **ALWAYS**
CALLING my name!
☺

I help them
GET TO PLACES
FASTER.

I TASTE THEIR FOOD
before they eat,
to make SURE
that it's <u>ALL RIGHT</u>.

I help them
LOOK FOR treasures
IN THE GARDEN.

I TRY TO
LOOK my best
FOR THEM.

NOOOO!

I warm THEIR BEDS
BEFORE they go to sleep.

I tidy up
THEIR
NEWSPAPERS.

If I am hungry,
I FEED MYSELF.

I help them
WITH THE LAUNDRY.

They must
<u>LOVE ME</u>
♥
VERY MUCH.

I LOVE them TOO!

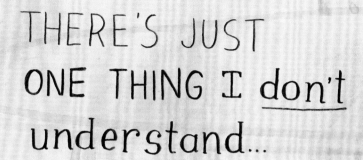

THERE'S JUST
ONE THING I don't
understand...

Why did they buy me
A COLLAR WITH THE
WRONG NAME ?

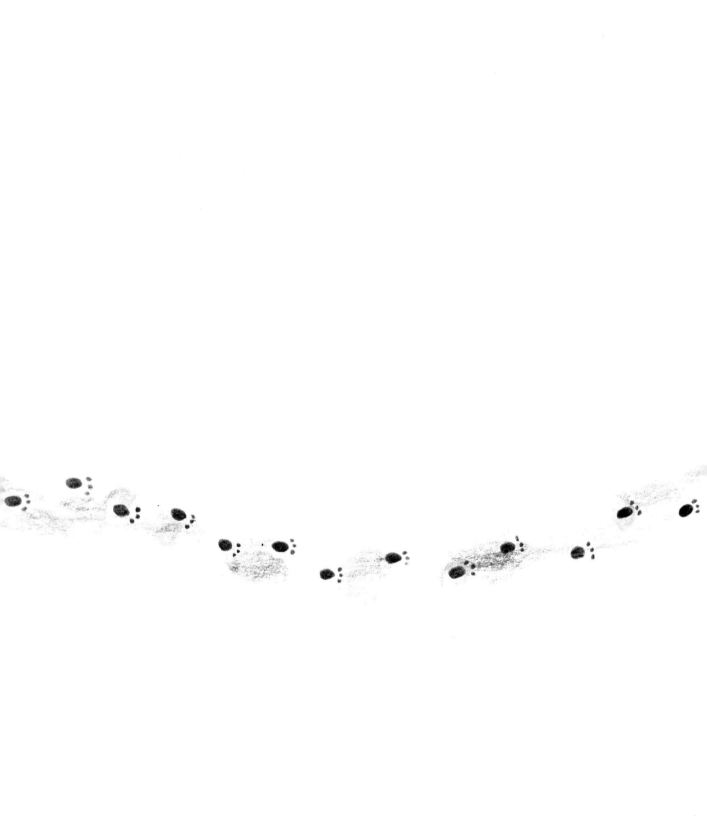